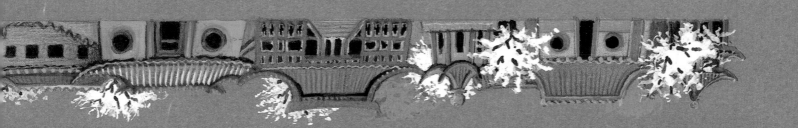

DIGGING TO
CHINA

For Morag and Nadia
and for Nan

Text and illustrations copyright © 1988 by Donna Rawlins
First American Edition 1989 published by Orchard Books

Orchard Books, A division of Franklin Watts, Inc.
387 Park Avenue South, New York, NY 10016

Orchard Books Canada
20 Torbay Road, Markham, Ontario 23P 1G6

First published in 1988 by Ashton Scholastic Pty Limited.
Manufactured in the United States of America
Book design by Mina Greenstein   10 9 8 7 6 5 4 3 2 1

The text of this book is set in 18 pt. Berkeley Oldstyle Medium.
The illustrations are watercolor and colored pencil.

Library of Congress Cataloging-in-Publication Data
Rawlins, Donna.   Digging to China / by Donna Rawlins.   p.   cm.
Summary: Hearing her friend Marj, the elderly lady next door, speak wistfully of China,
Alexis digs a hole all the way through the earth to that exotic country and brings back
a postcard for Marj's birthday.
ISBN 0-531-05814-X. – ISBN 0-531-08414-0 (lib. ed.)
[1. Holes–Fiction.   2. Old age–Fiction.]   I. Title.   PZ7.R1973Di   1989   [E]–dc19
89-42536   CIP   AC

DIGGING TO CHINA

Donna Rawlins

ORCHARD BOOKS   NEW YORK

A division of Franklin Watts, Inc.

LEXIS and Marj are very good friends. They both like the same things, especially cacti, which Marj gives to Alexis in tiny terra-cotta pots for her collection. Marj likes succulents: fleshy plants that hold water in their leaves and sometimes look more like strange little animals than plants.

 NE DAY, Alexis was sitting on the edge of Marj's garden while her friend was digging. Alexis saw a plant she had never seen there before. It had vivid red flowers that hung down like bells.

"What's that one?" she asked. "I like that one."

"It's a Chinese lantern plant," said Marj. "A Chinese lantern— it grows in China. That's a place I always wanted to visit. Sort of exotic, they say."

E XOTIC?" asked Alexis. "What's exotic?"

"You know, like Arab tents and elephants and giant tortoises. China would be exotic I think. It's a shame I've never been there, but now I'm too old for that sort of thing. If you ever go there you should send me postcard. I'd like to see China."

Marj looked a bit dreamy. She was remembering all the times she didn't go to China.

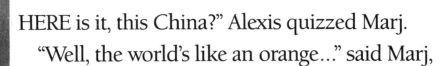

"HERE is it, this China?" Alexis quizzed Marj.

"Well, the world's like an orange…" said Marj, "round. China's on the other side, so if you dug a hole deep enough, you could go straight there."

"Really?" asked Alexis.

"Really," said Marj.

Marj was certain of this because her mother had told her, and her mother was always right. She had been to China and knew her way around the entire world. Alexis thought Marj's mother must have been exotic, too, just like China.

JUST then Bob called out from the back door.
Dinner was on the table.

"I'd better go. See you later Alex."

"See ya Marj."

Alexis hurried back through her garden, into her house, and straight to the bookshelves. She picked a big red book that had mostly pictures, and she looked in the back part called "Index." Marj had shown her how to read an index, and she searched the columns for "exotic."

"That's where I'll find China," she thought to herself. She ran her finger up and down the Es looking for "exotic." Alexis couldn't imagine how to spell it, so she looked at all the E words just to be sure.

LEXIS thought she'd check the whole index to see if exotic had been put in the wrong place. She started with A for aardvark, alligator, and anteater. Then she read all the Bs. After the Bs she began with the Cs. Halfway down the long list of words, she found a better word than exotic. "China...page 138."

She opened the book to page 138 and there, sure enough, was China. It looked exotic to Alexis, just as Marj and Marj's mother had said.

"That settles it," Alexis said out loud to herself. "I'm going there."

HE next day Alexis surveyed the back garden for the best place to dig. The spot by the fig tree looked as good as any and it was tucked away so that no one could see.

There was a little hole in the fence where Alexis could sometimes keep an eye on Marj. Alexis thought it might be a good idea to keep her trip a secret for the time being, just in case she wasn't allowed to go. China sounded like it was a long way, and Alexis imagined Marj might miss her.

IGGING was hard at first. Alexis had to get friendly with the spade. She knew this because Frank, her other neighbor, had laughed at her in a friendly way one day when he had seen her being clumsy with a shovel. Frank was good at digging and taught her a couple of tricks to make it easier. He called it being friendly with the spade.

She practiced a bit on some soft soil in a flower bed, and then began the serious business of digging to China.

IT TOOK many weeks. Soon most of her time was taken up not with digging but with climbing all the way back every night in time for dinner. Each day she set off down the hole with her friendly spade and dug a little more.

"Marj's birthday is very soon," Alexis thought. "I know because it's vacation and we always have the whole day together on her birthday. I hope she doesn't miss me if I'm away this year."

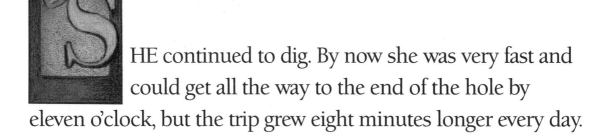HE continued to dig. By now she was very fast and could get all the way to the end of the hole by eleven o'clock, but the trip grew eight minutes longer every day.

ONE morning Alexis set off very early, without her spade. Instead she had gone to her piggy bank and taken out all the money she had saved. She tied it in the corner of her hanky and pushed it all the way down into her pocket.

Today was Marj's birthday. Alexis had to be back by dinner if she could.

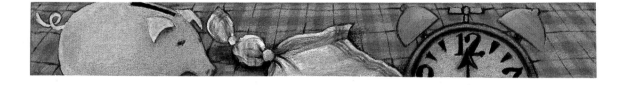

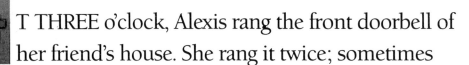T THREE o'clock, Alexis rang the front doorbell of her friend's house. She rang it twice; sometimes Marj has a cup of tea and a nap in the afternoon (she says she is old and tired).

Marj came to the door in her slippers and a birthday hat.

"Come in Alex," Marj invited loudly. "Come in and have some cake. It's my birthday."

"I know," said Alex. "I've brought you a surprise. I would have sent it to you but it seemed silly since I only live through the fence."

ARJ took the creamy envelope from Alex's out-stretched hand.

"Thank you Alex, a birthday card."

Marj slid the card slowly, slowly, out of the envelope.

She loved surprises, and she wanted to make this one last as long as possible. When finally she held the card up to the light to look at the picture, her eyes lit up like two stars.

"Oh, Alex," Marj beamed. "You shouldn't have. You bought me a postcard from China, how lovely. Look Bob, Alex bought me a postcard from China."

"HAT was China like?" Marj asked eagerly.

"Just like you said, Marj, exotic. You should go."

"I might after all, you know," said Marj.

Then they sat down on the back step with Bob and ate their cake, and talked about cacti and China for the rest of the day, while Alexis scraped the mud off her rubber boots with a stick.